Tara Binns
Double Choc Doc

Do amazing things!

by Lisa Rajan
Eerika Omiyale

When Tara Binns runs widdershins
Around the costume box,
The attic spins, the fun begins,
The magic clasp unlocks.

"Widdershins?
What's widdershins?"
Both you and Tara say,
It's when you run in circles
But go round the other way.

The box has big ideas,
And lots of hats and shoes,
It puts her in a costume
She wouldn't normally choose.

Each outfit brings adventure,
And takes her far away,
She shuts her eyes and wonders
"What will I be today?"

A doctor in a white coat,
She's looking very smart,
She checks her patient's pulse and
Has a listen to his heart.

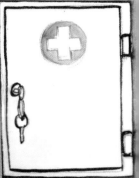

"What seems to be the problem?"
Says Tara to the lad,
"Tell me how you feel and
Any symptoms that you've had."

"My nose is really runny,
My throat feels very sore,
My temperature is rising
Way past one hundred and four."

"My bones feel very achy,
There's a throbbing in my head,
I'm sniffing and I'm sneezing
And I want to go to bed."

Tara said "You've got a cold,
A mild case of the flu,
Go home, wrap up, keep warm,
For there is nothing I can do."

The next boy was the same,
He was coughing, sniffing, wheezing,
"Please help me Dr Binns... I can't
Stop – Atchooo! ATCHOOO! – sneezing."

And patient after patient,
Came in to her and told
Of how they felt so awful
Because they had a cold.

SUPER TOMATO

Tara thought "Poor children —
A cold's no fun for sure,
So wouldn't it be wonderful
If I could find a cure?"

Tara closed the clinic and
Went on the internet,
She searched for 'common cold',
Got all the info she could get.

"It's caused by a virus,
And spread by coughs and sneezes,
And sadly it is one of
The incurable diseases."

One page said "The North Pole
Is the only place we know,
Where you cannot catch a cold,
Because of all the ice and snow."

"The temperature's too cold
For the cold virus to survive,
For when it gets all frozen up
It cannot stay alive."

She carried on researching,
Till her head began to ache,
She sneezed as she decided
It was time to take a break.

But walking to the bus stop
The sneeze turned into two,
A sniff, a cough, another sneeze
"Atchoo! Atchoo! ATCHOO!"

She started feeling gloomy,
And really quite unwell,
"I couldn't cure my patients' colds,
Now I've caught one as well."

She passed a small ice cream van,
A voice called "Hi, I'm Molly,
I know what would cheer you up –
A lovely orange lolly!"

Tara thought about it...
Mmmm... an ice cream would be nice,
And although it was Autumn time
She ordered a choc ice.

The choc ice made her mouth cold,
And her throat and tummy too,
She started feeling better,
Then an awesome idea grew.

"I think I've found the answer!
This stuff works like a dream,
We don't get colds in summer,
Because we eat ice cream."

"It makes our bodies colder,
Too cold for colds to live,
Staying warm is wrong — I now
Know just the thing to give."

"Take something very chilly,
That happens to be yummy,
And recreate the cold North Pole,
Inside each patient's tummy."

"We should work together,
We'd make a brilliant team,
We'll visit all my patients,
And give them an ice cream."

Molly beamed "I'd love to!
You're a very clever girl,
It would be great to help you,
Yes we should give it a whirl!"

They painted the ice cream van,
Green and yellow, red and white,
An ambulance with sprinkles on,
A very welcome sight.

They drove up every street,
To patients young and old,
Gave ice creams out to everyone,
And so cured every cold.

"I'm a really clever doctor,
My treatments are a dream,
Vanilla, Mint or Double Choc,
A big dose of ice cream!"

They drove up to a roundabout,
While heading home that day,
But instead of going clockwise they
Went round the other way.

The pavement started spinning,
She heard a loud KA-BOOM!
And next thing she was back home
In that dusty attic room.

She took the doctor's coat off,
And put back the stethoscope,
She thought of her adventure,
And was filled with pride and hope.

"I think that when I grow up,
Being a doctor's what I'll do,
I made people get better,
And discovered something new."

The chest replied "You kids should
Have ideas, big and small,
Be clever, be creative,
Make a better world for all."

When Tara Binns runs widdershins...

Tara Binns is a charming and clever little girl who finds an old chest in the attic that gives her a costume she wouldn't normally choose. With each costume comes a new job to do – and Tara has great fun rising to the challenges of each one. She solves problems, invents things and has brilliant ideas – and discovers how resourceful, practical and kind she can be along the way.

Tara's adventures show her that she can be or do anything – nothing is off limits and no jobs are just 'for boys' or 'for girls'. The Tara Binns books aim to inspire children, show them all the opportunities out there and plant big ideas in little minds.

Widdershins? What's widdershins?

It means taking a different path to the usual, or doing the opposite of what is expected. For Tara, who usually plays at being a princess, it opens her mind to exciting new ideas about jobs that often only boys dream about. The Tara Binns books aim to raise aspirations, counter gender stereotypes and provide a strong role model for girls and boys everywhere.

she gets to do amazing things!

Tara Binns
Crash Test Genius

by Lisa Rajan
Eerika Omiyale

In CRASH TEST GENIUS...
she becomes an engineer and a sudden accident gives her a brilliant idea that will make bumps, thumps, trips and falls a LOT more fun!

In EAGLE-EYED PILOT... she finds herself at the controls of a jumbo jet, and in avoiding a terrible thunderstorm happens upon what MIGHT be an old pirate treasure map.

Tara Binns
Eagle-Eyed Pilot

by Lisa Rajan
Eerika Omiyale

CAVENDISH ❄ KEBLE

Published by Cavendish Keble Ltd, 9 Perseverance Works,
Kingsland Road, London E2 8DD, UK. All rights reserved.
First published in 2015 in the United Kingdom.

A catalogue record for this book is available from the British Library.

ISBN 978-0-9930082-2-1
Text copyright © Lisa Rajan 2015
Illustrations copyright © Cavendish Keble Ltd 2015

For more copies of this book, please email: info@cavendishkeble.com
Printed in China